Scrambler
and the Snowy Rescue

Illustrations by Craig Cameron
Cover illustration by Dynamo

EGMONT

95% of the paper used in this book is recycled paper, the remaining 5% is an
Egmont grade 5 paper that comes from well managed forests. For more information
about Egmont's paper policy please visit www.egmont.co.uk/ethicalpublishing

EGMONT

We bring stories to life

First published in Great Britain 2008 by Egmont UK Limited
239 Kensington High Street, London W8 6SA

HiT entertainment

ISBN 978 1 4052 4057 4

1 3 5 7 9 10 8 6 4 2

Printed in Great Britain

When a snowstorm hits Sunflower Valley, it's Scrambler and Zoomer to the rescue! Will they work together and make it to the winter party in time?

One winter's day, Bob had gathered the team together. "I know you're all excited about the very first Sunflower Valley winter party, he began. "But first we have an important job to do."

"Ooh, what is it, Bob? Tell us!" said Dizzy.

"We're going to build a new concert hall, just like this one!" Bob told them. He pulled off a cover to reveal a big picture.

"It looks amazing. Yeah!" smiled Roley.

Just then, Scrambler arrived. "Hi Bob! Hi Wendy! Can I help?" he asked, excitedly.

"Thanks Scrambler, but we're all sorted," Bob replied.

Scrambler watched the others at work. He wished he could help with the party.

"Brrr, it's getting very cold," Dizzy shivered. "I wonder if it will snow?"

"I hope not," said Wendy. "It can make building very slippery and dangerous."

Meanwhile, Scoop had gone to help Bob's mum and dad, Robert and Dot, at the old yard. There was a new friend waiting to meet him.

"Scoop, meet R.Vee, my old building van!" smiled Robert.

"Hi, Scoop! Check out my roof box!" said the big blue van.

"Wow! R.Vee, you're amazing!" said Scoop.

"Let's go you two, we've got to collect a surprise from the mountains," said Dot.

Bob and the machines worked busily all day, until the frame of the hall was up.

"We should be finished in plenty of time for the party!" laughed Bob.

Suddenly, thick flakes of snow began to fall from the sky. "Wow!" giggled Dizzy. "Our first snow in Sunflower Valley!"

"Please keep snowing!" smiled Scrambler excitedly. "Lots of snow means lots of party jobs for Scrambler!"

The next morning, it had snowed so much that Wendy had to dig Bob out of his mobile home!

"We need Scoop and his snowplough to clear the roads," said Bob. "Or no one will be able to get to the party."

"But Scoop's in the mountains and his snowplough's down here," Wendy worried.

"I could take Scoop his snowplough! I'm great in the snow!" smiled Scrambler.

Scrambler revved his engine loudly, his wheels spun, and he whizzed straight into a snowdrift! "Brrr, chilly!" he shivered, when Bob had helped him out.

"Oh dear! It looks like you'll need some help," said Bob, picking up his talkie-talkie.

Soon, the noise of a helicopter buzzed above them in the sky.

The helicopter lowered its load to the ground, blowing snow everywhere!

"I've brought in someone very special to help us," said Bob. "It's Zoomer!"

"Who is Zoomer?" asked Scrambler.

"That's meeee! I'll get the snowplough to Scoop, for sure! I'm the best in the snow — ever!" boasted Zoomer, skidding up and down in the snow.

Scrambler was sad. "I wanted to fetch Scoop's snowplough," he sniffed.

"Hmm," said Bob. "Zoomer will need someone to show him the way up the mountains. Now who could do that?"

"I'll show him!" said Scrambler, eagerly.

"Good idea," said Bob. "But first you'll need some snow chains to stop your tyres slipping around in the snow."

"Wow! Wicked wheels!" smiled Scrambler, "Try and keep up with me, Zoomer!"

He set off, with Zoomer racing after him.

Up in the mountains, Scoop and R.Vee had collected the surprise for the party.

"All right! Let's hit the road!" roared R.Vee.

They turned on their engines, but their wheels skidded and spun on the icy road.

Scoop was worried. "I can't get us home without my snowplough," he cried.

Robert got out of R.Vee. "Oh dear, it looks like the road is blocked, too."

The snowplough was very heavy and Zoomer wheezed up the snowy hills. He was too proud to ask for help.

"Come on, we'll miss the party," Scrambler teased. Suddenly, his wheels skidded in the snow. "Woah!" Scrambler felt very silly.

"Maybe if we work together, we can get to Scoop quicker," Zoomer said, kindly.

Scrambler agreed and led the way up the steep slopes. Before long, the machines reached Scoop.

Scoop and R.Vee were very happy to see the little machines! Robert quickly fitted the snowplough, and Scoop led everyone through the snow to the party.

They arrived just in time! Everyone was there to greet them. Bob and the team had worked hard to finish the concert hall.

Robert and Bob unloaded the surprise from R.Vee's roof box. It was a big sack of presents for all the children to share!

"The hall looks brilliant!" said Zoomer and Scrambler together. "Perfect for a party!"

"Without you two there wouldn't have been a winter party at all!" said Bob.

"Well, I needed Zoomer's help!" said Scrambler, kindly.

"And I needed Scrambler's help! And together, we're a wicked winter team!" smiled Zoomer. "Zoom, Zoom!"

Start collecting your Bob the Builder Story Library NOW!

1 Bob and the Big Plan — ISBN: 978 1 4052 3142 8

2 Dizzy and the Talkie-Talkie — ISBN: 978 1 4052 3143 5

3 Scrambler and the Off-road Race — ISBN: 978 1 4052 3144 2

4 Wendy and the Surprise Party — ISBN: 978 1 4052 3140 4

RRP £2.99

5 Roley and the Woodland Walk — ISBN: 978 1 4052 3750 5

6 Benny and the Important Job — ISBN: 978 1 4052 3748 2

7 Sumsy and the Sunflower Spill — ISBN: 978 1 4052 3747 5

8 Muck and the Machine Convoy — ISBN: 978 1 4052 3749 9

9 Travis and the Tropical Fruit — ISBN: 978 1 4052 4110 6

10 Lofty and the Singing Stars — ISBN: 978 1 4052 4111 3

11 Scoop and the Bakery Build — ISBN: 978 1 4052 4108 3

12 Spud and the Funny Trees — ISBN: 978 1 4052 4109 0

My Bob the Builder Story Library is THE definitive collection of stories about Bob and the team. Look out for even more terrific titles coming soon!

A fantastic offer for Bob the Builder fans!

NOTE: Style of poster and door hanger may be different from those shown.

In every Bob the Builder Story Library book like this one, you will find a special token. Collect 4 tokens and we will send you a brilliant Bob the Builder poster and a double-sided bedroom door hanger!

Simply tape a £1 coin in the space above and fill out the form overleaf.

EGMONT

www.egmont.co.uk

To apply for this great offer, ask an adult to complete the details below and send this whole page with a £1 coin and 4 tokens, to:

BOB OFFERS, PO BOX 715, HORSHAM RH12 5WG

☐ Please send me a Bob the Builder poster and door hanger. I enclose 4 tokens plus a £1 coin (price includes P&P).

To be completed by an adult

Fan's name:

Address:

Postcode:

Email:

Date of birth:

Name of parent / guardian:

Signature of parent / guardian:

Please allow 28 days for delivery. Offer is only available while stocks last. We reserve the right to change the terms of this offer at any time and we offer a 14 day money back guarantee. This does not affect your statutory rights. Offers apply to UK only.

We may occasionally wish to send you information about other Egmont children's books, including the next titles in the Bob the Builder Story Library series. If you would rather we didn't, please tick ☐

Ref: BOB 004

cut along the dotted line and return this whole page